To read fluently is one of the basic aims of anyone learning English as a foreign language. **And it's never too early to start.** Ladybird Graded Readers are interesting but simple stories designed to encourage children between the ages of 6 and 10 to read with pleasure.

Reading is an excellent way of reinforcing language already acquired, as well as broadening a child's vocabulary. Ladybird Graded Readers use a limited number of grammatical structures and a carefully controlled vocabulary, but where the story demands it, a small number of words outside the basic vocabulary are introduced. In *Hansel and Gretel* the following words are outside the basic vocabulary for this grade:

cage, dead, drop, forest, light a fire, push, pieces, stepmother, stone, treasure, witch, woodcutter

Further details of the structures and vocabulary used at each grade can be found in the Ladybird Graded Readers leaflet.

A list of books in the series can be found on the back cover.

British Library Cataloguing in Publication Data
Ullstein, Sue
    Hansel and Gretel. —(English language teaching series).
    1. English language—Text-books for foreign speakers
    2. Readers—1950-
    I. Title   II. Dzierzek, Anna
    III. Grimm, Jacob. Hansel und Gretel   IV. Series
    428.6'4   PE1128
    ISBN 0-7214-1041-3

First edition

Published by Ladybird Books Ltd Loughborough Leicestershire UK
Ladybird Books Inc Lewiston Maine 04240 USA

Printed in England

Hansel and Gretel

written by Sue Ullstein
illustrated by Anna Dzierzek

Ladybird Books

Here are Hansel and Gretel.

Here is their father.
He is a woodcutter.

The children's mother
is dead. This is
their stepmother.
She is a bad woman.

9

The stepmother says,
"Hansel and Gretel
must go."

"No, no,"
the woodcutter says.
"No, no, no!"

"Yes, they must go,"
the stepmother says.
"We have no food for
them."

The woodcutter and the stepmother go to sleep. Hansel gets up. He goes out. He finds some little stones.

The next day the
stepmother says,
"Wake up, Hansel!
Wake up, Gretel! We
must get some wood."

They go into the forest. Hansel drops the little stones.

The woodcutter lights a fire.

"Stay here, children," he says. "We must find the wood now."

Hansel and Gretel are tired. They go to sleep. The woodcutter and the stepmother go home.

Hansel and Gretel
wake up. They find
the little stones.

''Look,'' Hansel says.
''Here are the little
stones. We can go
home now.''

Hansel and Gretel go home. The woodcutter is happy, but the stepmother is not happy.

Hansel and Gretel go
to bed.

The woodcutter says,
''Hansel and Gretel
must stay here. They
are my children.''

''No,'' the stepmother
says. ''We have no
food for them. They
must go.''

The woodcutter and the stepmother go to bed. Hansel gets up. He wants some little stones, but he cannot go out. He cannot open the door.

The next day the
stepmother says,
"Wake up, Hansel!
Wake up, Gretel! We
must get some wood."

They go into the
forest. Hansel
has no little stones.
He drops some little
pieces of bread,
but the birds eat
the bread.

The woodcutter lights
a fire.

''Stay here, children,''
he says. ''We must
find the wood now.''

Hansel and Gretel
are tired. They
go to sleep. The
woodcutter and the
stepmother go home.

Hansel and Gretel
wake up. They want
to go home, but they
cannot find the pieces
of bread. They cannot
go home.

Hansel and Gretel are hungry. They come to a house.

"Look at this house!" Gretel says. "We can eat it!"

They eat and eat.

A witch comes out.
She is a bad witch.
She wants to eat
Hansel and Gretel.
She puts Hansel into
a cage, and she takes
Gretel into her house.

The witch lights a fire.

"Is the fire hot?" she says.

"Yes, it is," Gretel says. "Look."

The witch looks into the fire. Gretel pushes her into the fire.

Gretel opens the cage.

"Hurry, Hansel!" she says. "We can go home now."

"Look!" Hansel says.
"Here's some treasure.
We can have it."

They go home. The woodcutter is happy.

''Your stepmother isn't here now,'' he says. ''You can stay. I'm very happy!''